KU-033-857

Shipwreck!

A first story about sorting and pairing

Written by Shen Roddie
Illustrated by Nadine Bernard Westcott

'Blistering Barnacles!' yelled Diver Dan
to Diver Dee. 'It's a Spanish shipwreck!'

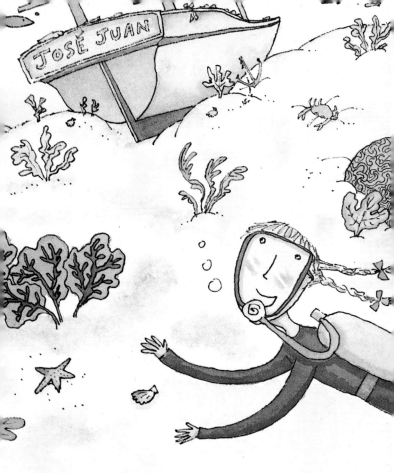

'So it is!' cried Diver Dee. 'Let's explore it!'

Diver Dan and Diver Dee swam round and round the José Juan.

'Isn't she magnificent!' they cried.
'I'll bet she's loaded with treasure!'
said Diver Dan.

He was right! There was so much treasure that it took Diver Dan and Diver Dee three days to bring it all up!

On the third day they finished loading it on to a trailer. Then they drove home.

'Now what do we do?' asked Diver Dee.
'Sort it out, of course!' said Diver Dan.

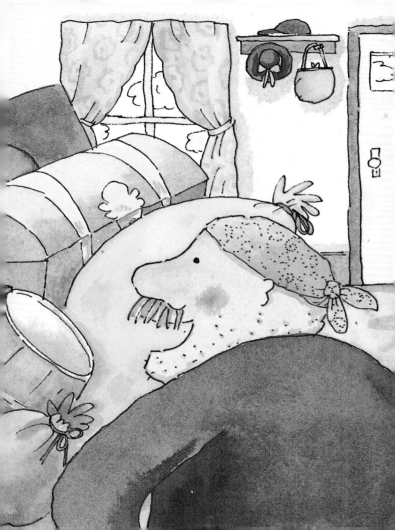

'Everything that glitters goes over here,' said Diver Dan. Into that pile went rings and necklaces and medals and rubies

and diamonds and emeralds and three
small mirrors.

'Not mirrors!' said Diver Dan.

'Why not? They glitter, don't they?' asked Diver Dee.

'Yes,' answered Diver Dan, 'but they're not precious, like the other things.'

'All useful tools into this pile,' said Diver Dan. In went a hammer, a saw, a drill, a shovel, a rake and a big pile of rope.

'Not rope!' cried Diver Dan.
'But rope is useful,' said Diver Dee.
'It certainly is,' said Diver Dan, 'but it's not a tool.'

'Anything that makes music in this pile!' said
Diver Dan. In went a ship's bell, a trumpet,
a Spanish guitar and pots and pans.
'Not pots and pans!' cried Diver Dee.
'They're kitchen things!'

'Not to me!' said Diver Dan.
'To me they're drums!'
BOOM! BANG! BOOM!

'Everything else over there!' said Diver Dan. Soon there was a huge heap.

'All done!' said Diver Dan.
'I'm tired. I'm off to bed!'

'Oh no, you're not!' cried Diver Dee. 'This pile is a mess! We'll have to pair up things if we want to sell them!'

Diver Dan yawned.
'Don't go to sleep! Let's sing as we work!'
said Diver Dee.

So they sang:

'Cup and saucer, fork and spoon,

gold and silver, telescope and moon.'

'Anchor and chain - we're nearing shore.

Cannon and balls - in case of war!'

'Toy bird and cage, fish and bowl,

needle and thread to sew up a hole.'

'Sock and shoe, coat and hat.

We can play with these - a ball and bat!'

Just then they heard a loud cry.
'WAAAAH!'

'Galloping octopus! It's a baby!' cried
Diver Dan.
'Where?' asked Diver Dee.
'There!' answered Diver Dan.

Then they both cried, 'It's a Merbaby!'

'We've carried her away by mistake!'
cried Diver Dee.
'Quick! Stop her crying!' cried Diver
Dan.
'How?' asked Diver Dee.
'Sing a lullaby! Baby goes with lullaby!'

So they sang:

'Rock-a-bye baby
from a wrecked boat.
When the storm breaks,
the cradle will float.'

Merbaby cried louder than ever!

'How about a bottle? Baby goes with bottle!' yelled Diver Dan.

They fetched a bottle with a little ship inside. But Merbaby pushed it away.

'Rattle! Baby goes with rattle!'
shouted Diver Dee.

Diver Dan strung three seashells together, clacketty-clack! But Merbaby screamed louder than ever!

Diver Dan and Diver Dee ran round the room with their hands over their ears. 'Think! Think! Think!' they bellowed. 'What else goes with baby?'

'There's only one thing left,' said Diver Dan.

'Baby goes with . . . Mother!'

Hurriedly, they bundled up Merbaby, got back into the car, and drove to the ocean.

They dived down, down, down to the José Juan.
'Mama!' gurgled Merbaby, smiling again.

Exhausted from their long day, Diver Dan and Diver Dee drove home. Before going to bed, they each paired soap with a towel.

Then they paired toothbrush with toothpaste, pyjama tops with pyjama bottoms, and candles with candlesticks.

'Dan?' whispered Diver Dee. 'What goes
with tired divers?'
'Zzzzzz,' came the reply.
'I guess I'll never know!' said Diver Dee,
as she drifted off to sleep.

For José Juan . . . S.R.

First Edition published 1997 by Reader's Digest Children's Books,
King's Court, Parsonage Lane,
Bath BA1 1ER
Copyright © 1997 Reader's Digest® Children's Books,
a subsidiary of The Reader's Digest Association, Inc.

READER'S DIGEST®, THE DIGEST and
the Pegasus logo are registered trademarks of
The Reader's Digest Association, Inc.
of Pleasantville, New York, USA

Manufactured in China